For Richard

Text copyright © 1990 by Mathew Price.
Illustrations copyright © 1990 by Atsuko Morozumi
Library of Congress catalog card number: 89–46577
Printed in Hong Kong
First American edition, 1990
Sunburst edition, 1993
Second printing, 1995

ONE
GORILLA

A Counting Book

Atsuko Morozumi

A Sunburst Book
Farrar, Straus & Giroux

Here is a list of things I love.
One gorilla.

Two butterflies among the flowers and one gorilla.

Three budgerigars in my house
and one gorilla.

Four squirrels in the woods
and one gorilla.

Five pandas in the snow
and one gorilla.

Six rabbits in a field
and one gorilla.

Seven frogs by the fence
and one gorilla.

Eight fish in the sea
and one gorilla.

Nine birds among the leaves
and one gorilla.

Ten cats in my garden
and one gorilla.

10 cats

9 birds

8 fish

7 frogs

6 rabbits

5 pandas

4 squirrels

3 budgerigars

2 butterflies

But where is my gorilla?

Ah, there he is.